THE GIZMOS' PARTY

Paul Shipton
Illustrated by Nigel Sandor

RIGBY

Chapter 1

One day, I was playing a game of football with my friends. Suddenly, the alarm on my hologram phone buzzed. I groaned and clicked it on. A hologram of my mum's face appeared. My friends thought it was amazing.

Then my mum began speaking. "Albert Gizmo, come home right now for dinner!"

It was no good arguing. I headed home and missed the end of the game.

Sometimes life is hard when your mother is an inventor.

The hologram phone was Mum's latest invention. Everyone thought it was brilliant, but I was fed up with Mum's strange gadgets. Sometimes I wished I had normal parents.

My sister, Marie, felt the same way.

"Why can't they have normal hobbies like stamp collecting or deep-sea diving?" she asked that evening.

"Or ballroom dancing or alligator wrestling?" I said.

We both stared at the hologram phone on the coffee table.

"I hate this thing," I said as I turned a dial on the machine. It came off in my hand. "Oops."

What should we do? Mum hates it when we touch her inventions. I stuck the dial back on as quickly as possible. I hoped it wasn't broken.

Just then, Mum came back in the room.

"Your dad's favourite film is on TV tonight," she said. "I must call him and tell him that *Invaders from Planet Zed* is on." She turned the machine on and punched in Dad's number.

Marie and I looked at each other
nervously. Would the machine still work?

"It's time to come home and watch your
favourite film on TV," Mum said into
the phone.

I let out a sigh of relief. It looked as if
the machine still worked.

I was wrong. I *had* broken the phone. Dad's hologram phone buzzed, but he didn't get Mum's message. Someone else got the message instead.

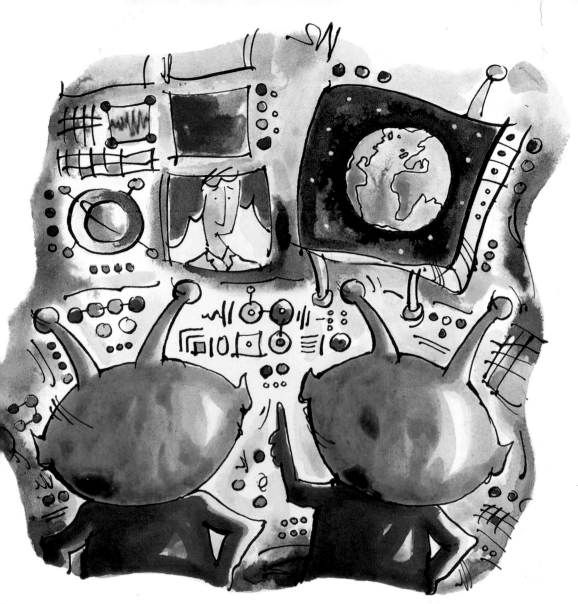

Far, far away, two strange figures
were listening.

"Interesting," said one. "What is a film?"

"And what is TV?" asked the other.

"Interesting."

Chapter 2

Back at home, Mum was getting worried.

"The film is starting," she said. "Where's your dad?"

The doorbell rang. Marie answered it.

The next thing I heard was her screaming.

Two aliens were at the door. I've seen lots of alien films, so I knew these were the real thing.

"We have come to watch something called a film," said one.

"On something called a TV," added the other.

What do you say when visitors from
another planet are at the door?

"Er . . . come in," I said. "But remember
to wipe your feet."

Of course, Mum and Marie were surprised, but the aliens seemed very friendly.

"W-why are you here?" asked Mum. She looked shocked but excited.

"We were watching your planet when we got your message," said one alien.

"The one about TV," said the other.

I took the hint and turned the TV on. We all looked at the screen in horror. It was the scene from the film where the human hero zaps the aliens. Unfortunately, the aliens in the film looked a lot like the aliens in our living room. Oops!

I tried to smile, but the aliens looked really angry.

"This is terrible!" shouted one.

"You call that entertainment? What sort of planet is this?" asked the other.

Mum tried to explain, but they just wouldn't listen.

I was worried the aliens might zap **us**. Suddenly, I remembered the remote control in my hand. I switched to the video channel. A music video was playing.

As soon as they heard the music, the aliens froze. They looked at the screen in amazement.

And then they began dancing . . .

Well, I *think* it was dancing. They sort of jumped around the room, waving their arms and giggling.

When the song was over, one alien gasped, "We never knew your Earth music was so . . . "

"Interesting," said the other.

The first alien looked at us and demanded, "Why aren't you dancing?"

We didn't want to get them angry again, so we joined in.

When the music video was over, we danced to Marie's CDs. When Dad got home, we were still dancing. We were tired, but we didn't want the aliens to think we were rude.

At last, the visitors said that they had to go. We all tried to hide our relief. At the door, they stopped and turned around.

"Before this evening, we were going to destroy your planet," said one.

"But we have decided not to," said the other. "Your music is too . . . interesting."

Before they disappeared in their spaceship, they waved and shouted, "We'll see you next week for another party!"